Hans
in Luck

Retold from the
BROTHERS GRIMM
by
PAUL
GALDONE

Parents Magazine Press • New York

Library of Congress Cataloging in Publication Data

Galdone, Paul.
    Hans in luck.
    SUMMARY: When his seven years' wages in gold proves
too heavy, Hans trades it for one thing after another until
he arrives home empty-handed but convinced he is a lucky man.
    [1. Fairy tales. 2. Folklore — Germany] I. Grimm,
Jakob Ludwig Karl, 1785-1863. Hans im Glück. II. Title.
PZ8.G127Han   398.2'1'0943 [E]   79-16154
ISBN 0-8193-1011-5 ISBN 0-8193-1012-3 lib. bdg.

Hans had worked seven years
for his master.
"Now it is time to go
see my mother," he said.

So his master said,
"You have served me well.
Here is your pay."
And he gave Hans a lump of gold
almost as big as his head.

Hans tied the lump
in his handkerchief,
slung it over his shoulder,
and set off for home.

As he plodded along
with his heavy load,
he met a man
riding a lively horse.

"Oh!" cried Hans. "How fine
it must be to ride at ease
instead of stumbling over stones
with this lump of gold!"

The man said, "I will give you
my horse if you will give me
your lump of gold in exchange."
"With all my heart," said Hans.
"But I warn you it is heavy."

The horseman got off the horse,
took the gold, and helped Hans up.
Then he said, "When you want
to go fast, click your tongue
and say, 'GEE-UP!'"

Hans rode off glad at heart.
As he went along, he thought
he would like to go faster.
So he began to click his tongue
and say, "GEE-UP!"

The horse broke into a gallop.
Before Hans knew it,
he ended up in a ditch.

Luckily, a farmer who was walking
along the road with a cow caught
the horse before he got away.
Hans pulled himself to his feet,
feeling sore.

"I'll never ride a horse again that
tries to break my neck," he said.
"I'd rather walk slowly behind a cow
like yours who gives milk, butter,
and cheese every day."

"Well, now," said the farmer.
"I don't mind doing you a favor.
I'll gladly trade my cow
for your horse."

Hans agreed joyfully.
The farmer jumped on the horse,
wished Hans good day,
and soon rode out of sight.

Driving his cow quietly before him,
Hans thought of the lucky bargain
he had made.

"Now I shall always have butter
and cheese for my bread,
and milk to drink when I'm thirsty.
What more could I wish for?"

The noonday sun grew hotter
and the road lay hot ahead.
Hans grew very thirsty.
So he tied up the cow and tried to
milk her into his leather cap.

But not a drop of milk came.
Instead, the cow kicked him
and he fell to the ground.

A butcher who was coming along
with a pig stopped.
"What is the matter?" he asked.
Hans wasted no time telling him.

"Have a drink from my flask,"
said the butcher.
"How would you like to trade in
that old cow for a fat young pig?"

"Heaven reward such kindness!"
cried Hans as he handed over
his cow and took the pig's leash.

Hans jogged along with the pig,
thinking how lucky he was.

After a while he met a man
carrying a fine white goose.
The goose man seemed friendly,
so Hans told him all about
his lucky bargains.

The man told him he was
taking his goose to market.
"Feel how heavy it is!"
"Yes, very fine," said Hans.
"But my pig is nice and fat, too."

Then the man glanced around
and whispered to Hans,
"I want to warn you that
your pig may get you in trouble.
I just heard that a pig was stolen
in the next village. Everyone
is out looking for the thief."

Poor Hans grew pale with fright.
"For Heaven's sake, help me.
I am a stranger here.
Take my pig and give me your goose."

"To help you stay out of trouble
I will," said the goose man.
And he drove the pig away.

Lucky Hans went on his way
with the goose under his arm,
thinking how pleased
his mother would be.

When Hans was almost home
he saw a knife-grinder
singing as he worked.
Hans watched him a while.
At last Hans said,
"You must be well off.
You seem so happy at your work."

"Yes," said the man.
"My work pays well.
If you want money in your pocket,
you should grind knives—like me.
Hand over your goose, and I'll
give you a fine grindstone."

"I would be the happiest man
in the world if I always had
money in my pocket.
Here is my goose."

And the man gave him
an old stone from his cart.

Hans carried off the stone.
His eyes sparkled with joy.
"Everything I wish for
is mine," he said.

The stone was very heavy.
Hans went along slowly until
at last he came to a well.

He laid the stone on the edge
of the well and stooped down
for a drink of cool water.

As he leaned over to drink,
he happened to give the stone
a little push, and it splashed
into the well.

Hans jumped for joy as it sank.
He was so glad to be rid of
the heavy stone. "Nobody was
ever so lucky as I," he cried.

So on he went, carefree, till
he reached his mother's house.
Then he happily told her
of his good fortune.

ABOUT THE ARTIST

PAUL GALDONE came to the United States when he was fourteen. His own language, Hungarian, wasn't much help in talking to his high school classmates, so he quickly learned English. And in the meantime, he used his skills in a third "language"—drawing—to bridge the gap. After art school, he joined the staff of a New York publisher. It was there that he grew to love book production, and set off on his own, eventually turning to book illustration.

Some 275 picture books later (including two Caldecott Honor Books), Paul Galdone is without doubt a master of folktale art. To the two PARENTS books he has illustrated — Kathleen Leverich's *The Hungry Fox and the Foxy Duck* and Anne Rose's *The Talking Turnip*—he now adds a writing credit with his own sprightly version of this Grimm Brothers' tale.

Mr. Galdone and his wife live part of the year in New City, New York, and the other part in Tunbridge, Vermont.

A